To
the real
Otto

All rights reserved. Published

in the United States by Random House

Children's Books, a division of Penguin Random

House LLC, New York. • Random House and the colophon

are registered trademarks of Penguin Random House LLC. • Visit

us on the Web! rhcbooks.com • Educators and librarians, for a variety of teaching

tools, visit us at RHTeachersLibrarians.com • *Library of Congress Cataloging-in-Publication Data:*

Name: Cummings, Troy, author, illustrator. • Title: Otto the ornament / written, illustrated, and festooned

by Troy Cummings. • Description: First edition. | New York : Random House Children's Books, [2023] |

Audience: Ages 3–7. | Summary: Initially, a super-snazzy Christmas tree ornament, Otto, thinks he should be placed

at the top of the tree to be admired, but then he realizes where he really wants to be. • Identifiers: LCCN 2022033820 (print) |

LCCN 2022033821 (ebook) | ISBN 978-0-593-48120-2 (trade) | ISBN 978-0-593-48121-9 (lib. bdg.) |

ISBN 978-0-593-48122-6 (ebook) • Subjects: LCSH: Christmas tree ornaments—Fiction. | Belonging—Fiction. |

Christmas—Fiction. | LCGFT: Christmas fiction. | Picture books. • Classification: LCC PZ7.C91494 Ot 2023 (print) |

LCC PZ7.C91494 (ebook) | DDC [E]—dc23 • Random House Children's Books supports the First Amendment and celebrates the right to read.

MANUFACTURED IN CHINA

10 9 8 7 6 5 4 3 2 1

First Edition

OTTO the ORNAMENT

Written, illustrated, and festooned by

Troy Cummings

Random House 🏠 New York

It was
the night
before
the night
before
Christmas.

A jumble of happy ornaments were nestled
all snug in their tree,

singing songs . . . playing games . . .
and mostly just, you know,
hanging around.

Life for the ornaments
was peaceful and calm.

Until the new guy showed up.

"Welcome to the family!"
sang a green glass bell.

"Sweet to meet you!"
called a candy cane.

"Ho-ho-hoooope you like it here!"
laughed a wooden Santa. "There's
a jolly branch for you, right in the
middle of our tree!"

"The middle? Um. There must
be some kind of mistake," said
Otto, scratching his cap.

"But a superstar like me belongs on the top of the tree,"
said Otto. "I'm snazzy! I'm jazzy! I'm Christmas-pizzazzy!"

{ Sleighbell
Silver }

{ Sugarplum
Purple }

{ Mistletoe
Green }

{ Cranberry
Red }

{ Candle Flame
Gold }

{ Sparkly Snow
Glitter }

Otto did a little dance on the carpet,
getting glitter everywhere.

"Scooch aside, trinkets, so I can make
my way to the top!"

The ornaments looked down at Otto.
But nobody scooched.

Otto's hook drooped.

"Aw, chestnuts!" he said. "I don't need you!
I'll go find my *own* tree!"

And so he did. With a flick of his
ribbon, Otto bobbled out the doggy
door and into the snowy night.

The first tree he tried was too tall.

The second tree was too small.

But the third tree was jusssssst . . .

Otto spun around town, trying every tree he could find.

"Aw, frankincense!"
said Otto. "None of those
trees were right for me!"
And that's when he saw
the light.

"Sweet Blitzen!" said Otto. "A Christmas festival!"

It was the ritziest, glitziest party Otto had ever seen. There was food and music and ice-skating and eggnog.

And towering above it all: a spectacular Christmas tree made entirely of lights.

Otto's eyes grew wide and sparkly.

"O holy night," he whispered. "I've found my tree!"

Otto swung his way up the twinkling tree. He teetered at the top, beaming at the crowd below.

But nobody looked up. They were too busy singing songs, playing games, and mostly just, you know, hanging around.

Otto blinked. On the outside, he looked merry and bright. But on the inside? He felt . . . hollow.

"What's the point of being at the top if I don't have anyone to share it with?" he said to himself.

He lowered his head.

His hook drooped.

And what happened next was a total shock.

Otto had hit rock bottom.

His hook was bent.

His ribbon was missing.

His cap was dented.

His side was cracked.

And his snazzy, jazzy paint had almost been scraped away.

"Aw, humbug," Otto moaned. "Now I'm so plain . . .
so ordinary. . . . I'm a mess!"

And that's when he noticed something else in the darkness.
Something dirty. And ragged. And lost.

"A mitten?" said Otto. "How did you wind up in the gutter?"

The mitten rubbed against Otto and purred.

Otto gasped. "Jumping jingle bells! I know exactly where you belong!"

Otto used his hook
to help the mitten climb
from the gutter.

Then they hitched a ride home.

Otto rolled back into the living
room with his mitten in tow.

"Otto? Is that you?" said
the green glass bell.

"You look a bit rattled,"
said the candy cane.

"And who's your woolly
friend?" asked the wooden
Santa. "She looks familiar!"

Otto looked down at the floor.
"I'm sorry I've been such a lump
of coal to you all," he said. "But I
had to come back! I knew this lost
little mitten would feel right at
home in your tree."

"I think you mean *our* tree,"
said a gingerbread bear.

With a loop of tinsel, the ornaments lifted
Otto and the mitten onto the tree.

PURRRR

The mitten scampered
over to her partner.

They each gave Otto
a big thumbs-up.

And Otto did something he'd never done before.

There, in the glow of the light,

he closed his eyes . . .

he took a breath . . .

. . . and he reflected.

His shiny silver surface
showed what was special about
each of his friends.

Otto wasn't at the top of
the tree.

He was in the middle,
surrounded by his new family.

Right where he belonged.

TROY CUMMINGS is the creator of the *New York Times* bestseller *Can I Be Your Dog?* and its companion books, *I Found a Kitty!* and *Is This Your Class Pet?* He has written and illustrated a sleighload of other children's books, including *The Eensy Weensy Spider Freaks Out! (Big-Time!)*, *Little Red Gliding Hood* (written by Tara Lazar), *Those Are Not My Underpants!* (written by Melissa Martin), and the chapter-book series The Notebook of Doom. He lives in Greencastle, Indiana, with his messy kids and neat cats. Check out more of Troy's work at troycummings.net.